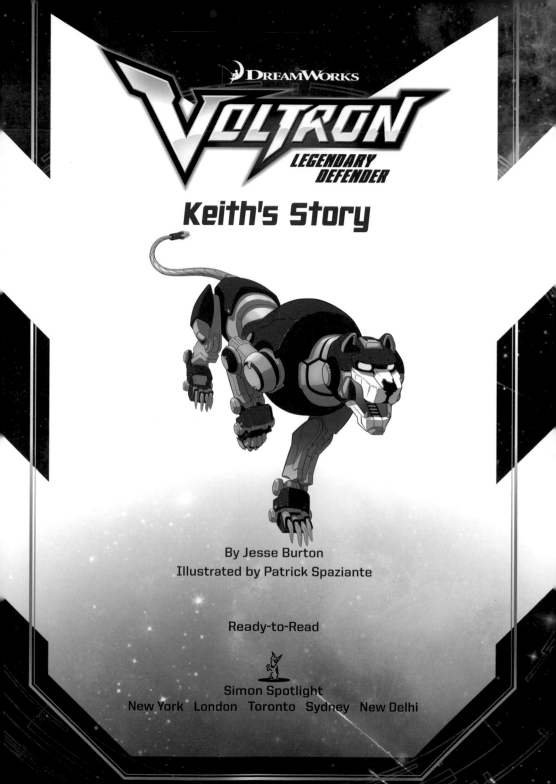

VOLTRON
LEGENDARY DEFENDER

Keith's Story

By Jesse Burton

Illustrated by Patrick Spaziante

Ready-to-Read

Simon Spotlight
New York London Toronto Sydney New Delhi

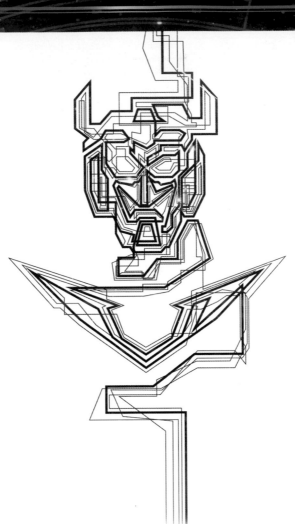

SIMON SPOTLIGHT
An imprint of Simon & Schuster Children's Publishing Division
1230 Avenue of the Americas, New York, New York 10020
This Simon Spotlight edition August 2018

 For information about
special discounts for bulk purchases, please contact Simon & Schuster Special Sales at
1-866-506-1949 or business@simonandschuster.com.
Manufactured in the United States of America 0718 LAK
2 4 6 8 10 9 7 5 3 1
ISBN 978-1-5344-2041-0 (hc)
ISBN 978-1-5344-2040-3 (pbk)
ISBN 978-1-5344-2042-7 (eBook)

Hey. My name is Keith.
I don't like to talk about myself, but
this is the story of how I became
part of team Voltron.
I pilot the Red Lion.

On Earth, I was the best pilot at a school called the Galaxy Garrison. Then I got kicked out. I didn't mind being on my own. I have been alone ever since I was little.

I quickly found a home in the desert.
I know this sounds strange,
but I was drawn to that place
and to an energy I felt there.

Then my friend Shiro crashed an alien space vessel nearby. Shiro was the first human to ever meet aliens, so the Garrison wanted to lock him up to study him. I couldn't let that happen.

I rescued Shiro with the help of three other students, named Hunk, Lance, and Pidge.

Later I showed them a cave I had found with walls covered in ancient drawings of lions.

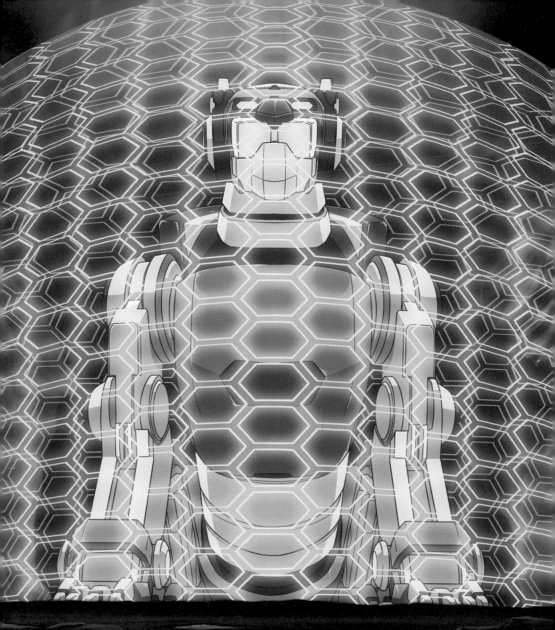

The drawings led us to a spaceship
called the Blue Lion.

We discovered that the Blue Lion was one of five lions that join together to form Voltron. With Voltron, we might be able to defeat the Galra and their evil leader, Zarkon!

The Blue Lion took us to a planet called Arus, where we met Princess Allura and her advisor, Coran. Allura helped us find the other lions.

Shiro, Lance, Pidge, and Hunk
each bonded with a lion.
I bonded with the Red Lion and
became its Paladin, or pilot.
We actually have a lot in common.

The Red Lion can move fast
but also has a bit of a temper.
I bet the Garrison teachers would
say the same about me!

I loved flying in the Red Lion,
but it wasn't easy for me to learn to
be on a team.
Pidge had amazing computer skills.
Hunk talked a lot.
I didn't know where I fit in.

If that weren't bad enough, Lance seemed to have a problem with me even when we got stuck in an elevator on the way to the pool.

Shiro told me that
"patience yields focus."
He was right.
After a while we all became friends,
and now we would do anything for
one another. They are the closest
thing I have to a family.

Even so, I didn't share everything about my past with them.
I had been hiding a strange blade.
I had had it my whole life and thought it might have something to do with my parents.

Then I met an alien named Ulaz.
He was part of a group called the
Blade of Marmora.
Its members were Galra aliens who
secretly worked against Zarkon.

His blade had the same symbol as mine!
I wondered if I was somehow connected to the Galra rebels and putting my team in danger.

Shiro and I flew the Red Lion to the home base of the Blade of Marmora.

Kolivan, the leader of the group, accused me of stealing the blade and ordered us to leave.

I asked Kolivan where my blade came from, but he wouldn't answer my questions.

Instead, he challenged me to the trials of Marmora.

He said if I survived, I could keep the blade and learn the truth.

In the first trial, I fought against just one fighter.
It wasn't easy, but I won!

I ran through a doorway to a trial where I fought two fighters.
Each doorway led me to more and more fighters.
It seemed like it would never end.

Then I walked through a door that
led me into a kind of dream.
My father was in the dream too.
He told me that my blade had
belonged to my mother.
I wanted to know more, but then
I woke up.

After all that, Kolivan still did not want to let me keep my blade. When I handed it over, something amazing happened.

The symbol on the blade glowed.
"The only way this is possible
is if you have Galra blood in
your veins!" Kolivan said.

If what Kolivan said was true,
it meant I could be part alien!

I began to wonder if I belonged with the Blade of Marmora instead of with the Paladins.
It really made things confusing just when I was starting to feel like part of the team!

Then I realized that no matter where I came from, we were all on the same team.

I still don't have all the answers, but I hope to learn more as we work together to save the universe from Zarkon!